Forces

PHYSICAL SCIENCE

Sandy Sepehri

Bethany, Missouri

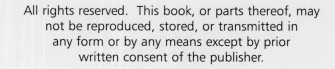

Photo Credits:
Cover © Fielding Piepereit; Title Page © Rose Hayes; Page 4 © Okapi Studio; Page 5 © Karen Town; Page 6 © Piotr Przeszlo; Page 7 © Ufuk ZIVANA; Page 9 © Bonnie Jacobs; Page 11 © Fielding Piepereit; Page 12 © Paul Mckeown; Page 13 © Dan Wilton; Page 15 © Kenneth C. Zirkel; Page 17 © Jane Norton; Page 18 © Jamie Wilson; Page 19 © NASA; Page 21 © Sean Locke; Page 22 © DigitalVision

Cataloging-in-Publication Data

Sepehri, Sandy
    Forces / Sandy Sepehri — 1st ed.
    p. cm. — (Physical science)

    Includes bibliographical references and index.
    Summary: Text and photographs introduce the physical science of
force, from what it is, to how it plays a part in everyday life.
    ISBN-13: 978-1-4242-1414-3 (lib. bdg. : alk. paper)
    ISBN-10: 1-4242-1414-9 (lib. bdg. : alk. paper)
    ISBN-13: 978-1-4242-1504-1 (pbk. : alk. paper)
    ISBN-10: 1-4242-1504-8 (pbk. : alk. paper)

    1. Force and energy—Juvenile literature. [1. Force and energy.]
I. Sepehri, Sandy. II. Title. III. Series.
    QC73.4.S47 2007
    531'.6—dc22

First edition
© 2007 Fitzgerald Books
802 N. 41st Street, P.O. Box 505
Bethany, MO 64424, U.S.A.
Printed in China
Library of Congress Control Number: 2006940881

Table of Contents

What Is Force?

To brush your teeth, you need a toothbrush, toothpaste, water, and something else. You also need **force**. Force is a push or a pull upon something.

The force of your muscles moves your toothbrush up and down.

People make forces and so do machines.

There are forces in nature. The force of the wind moves this flag.

Moving Forces

All forces have to do with how people and things move. A thing will not move, unless a force makes it move. Your pillow can't be in a pillow fight unless you use force to swing it!

9

Large Mass

Force

Force

Small Mass

Force

The more **mass** something has, the more force it takes to move it.

It takes extra force to pull this wagon with the dog in it.

Once something starts moving, there has to be a force to make it stop.

Friction stops
objects moving

The force that makes this skateboard stop
is called **friction**. The friction between the
wheels and the sidewalk makes the skateboard
stop moving.

Things move in the same direction of the force against them. Forces can be added together. The force of two people makes it easier to push the car.

Force

Balanced Forces

Forces can be balanced. These kids are using the same amount of force, but in opposite directions. So, their force is balanced.

Force

Force

Gravity

What makes the water curve down? It's **gravity**. Gravity is the force that pulls things toward the Earth. Without gravity, the water would float away.

Force of Gravity

Gravity is a force that pulls things toward the Earth.

Forces can be measured. The limes' weight shows the force of gravity upon it.

Gravity makes the limes weigh
two pounds.

This boy uses different forces to swing. Can you name them?

Glossary

force (FORS) — a push or pull upon something

friction (FRICK shun) — a force between things that are touching, making it harder for things to slide past each other

gravity (grav EH tee) — the force that pulls things towards the Earth

mass (MASS) — size and weight of an object, "how heavy" something is

Index

FURTHER READING

Greenberg, Daniel. *Amusement Park Science*. Chelsea Clubhouse, 2003.
Parker, Steve. *Forces and Motion*. Chelsea House Publishers, 2005.
Sonneborn, Liz. *Forces in Nature*. Rosen Publishers, 2005.

WEBSITES TO VISIT

Because Internet links change so often, Fitzgerald Books has developed an online list of websites related to the subject of this book. This site is updated regularly. Please use this link to access the list: www.fitzgeraldbookslinks.com/ps/for

ABOUT THE AUTHOR

Sandy Sepehri is an honors graduate from the University of Central Florida. She has authored several children's books and is a columnist for a parents' magazine.